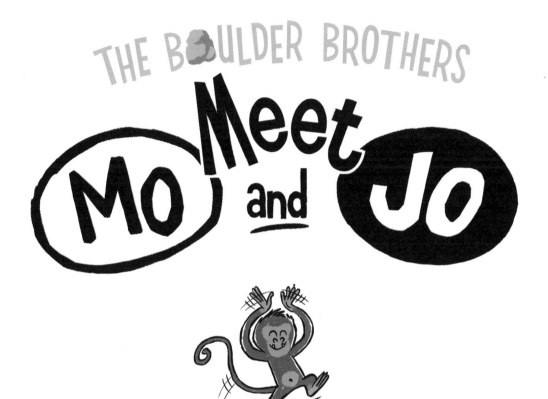

THE BOULDER BROTHERS Meet Mo and Jo

A **JuMp•into•CHAptErs** Book

Text Copyright © 2014 Sarah Lynn Scheerger
Illustrations Copyright © 2014 Pierre Collet-Derby
All rights reserved/CIP data is available.
Published in the United States 2014 by
🍎 Blue Apple Books, 515 Valley Street,
Maplewood, NJ 07040
www.blueapplebooks.com
Printed in China
First Edition 11/14

Hardcover ISBN: 978-1-60905-501-1
Paperback ISBN: 978-1-60905-561-5

2 4 6 8 10 9 7 5 3 1

Does Mo smell better?

Mo sniffs. Jo sniffs. The stink is still there!

Is Mo right about Jo?

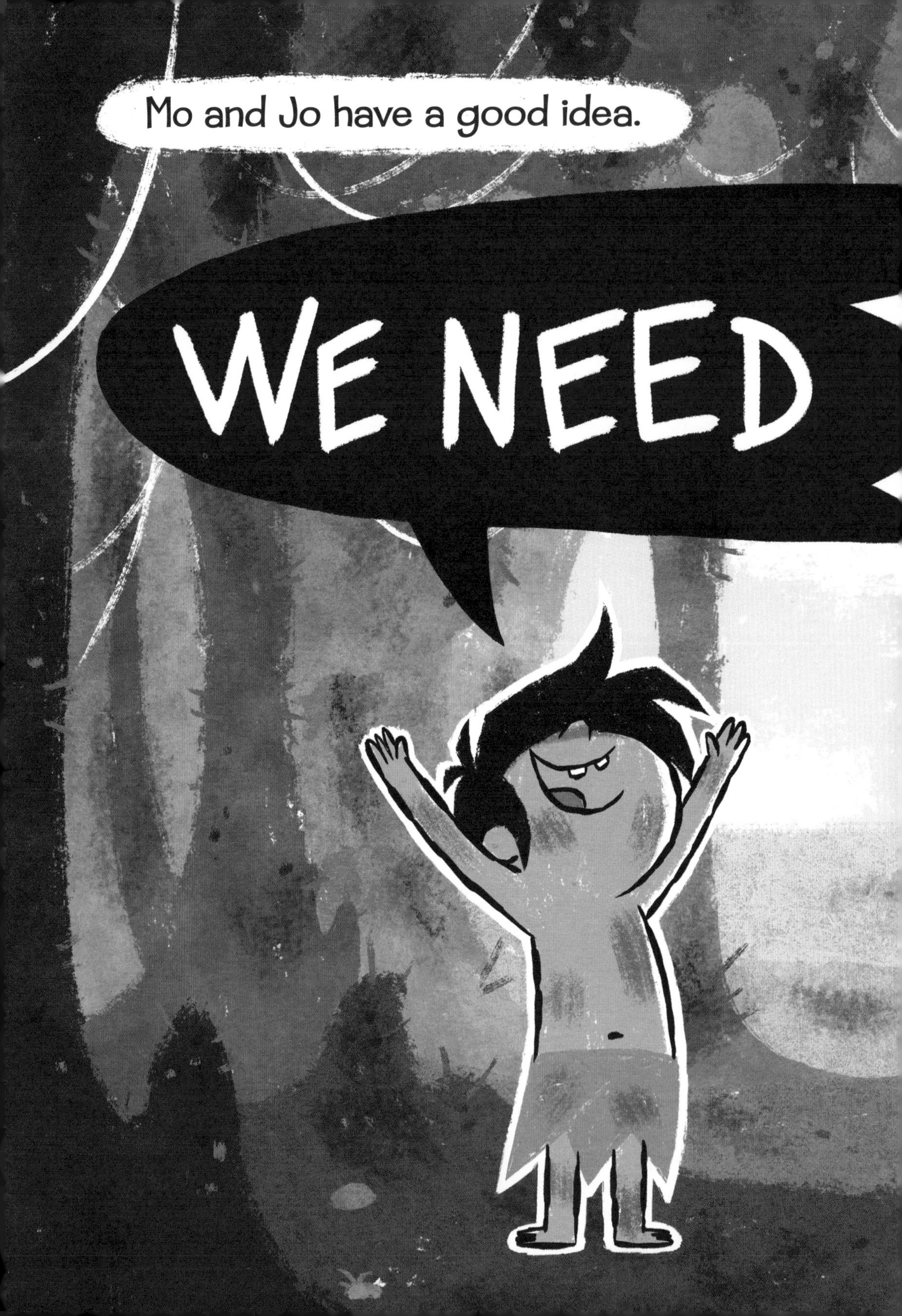
Mo and Jo have a good idea.
WE NEED

Mo and Jo have not
had a bath in a long time.

Jo smells good. Mo smells good.
But the stink is not gone.

They find out what stinks.

Mo and Jo know what to do.

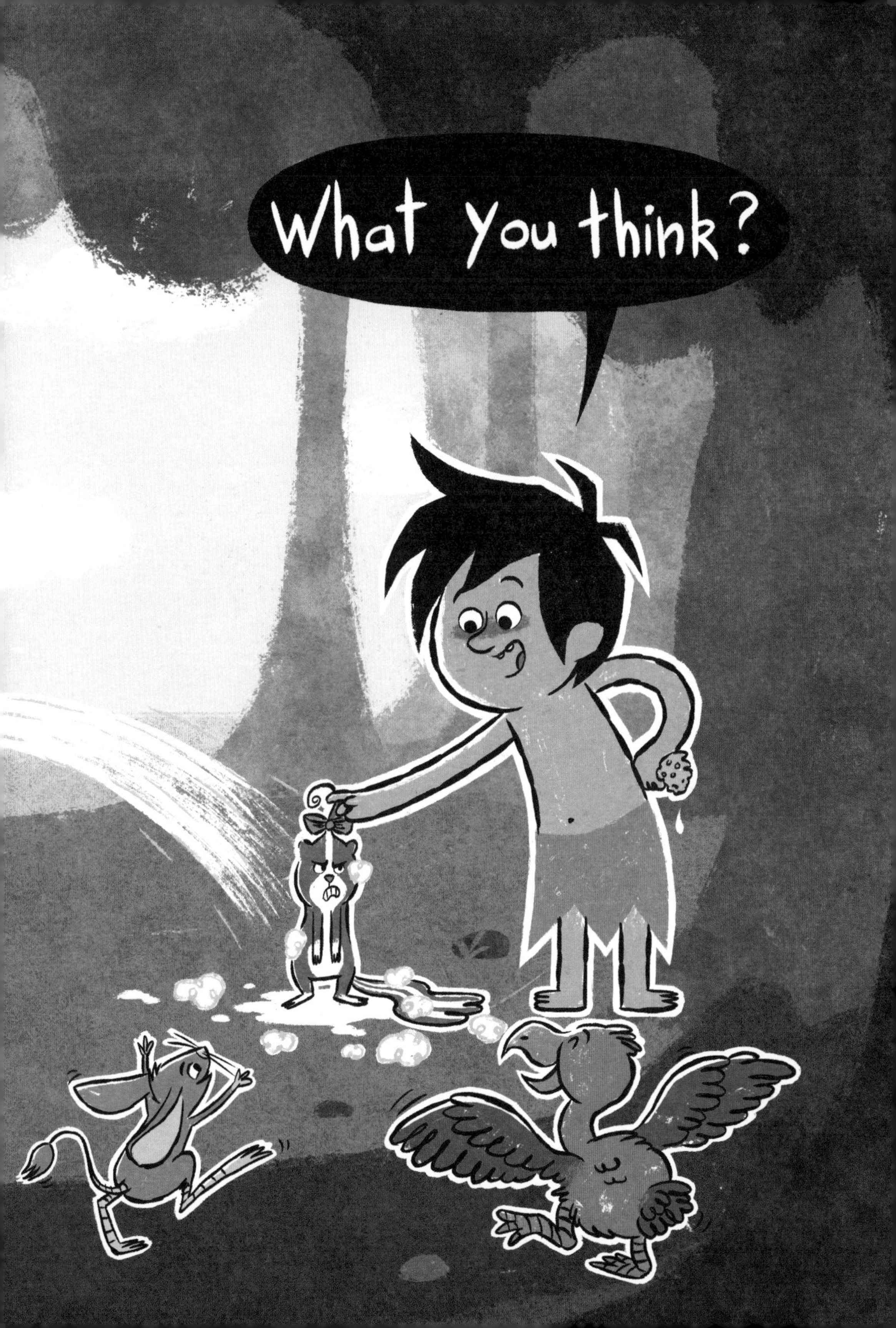
What you think?

The skunk liked the stink.
Can Mo and Jo run faster than the skunk?

CHAPTER 2:
HIDE
AND PEEK!

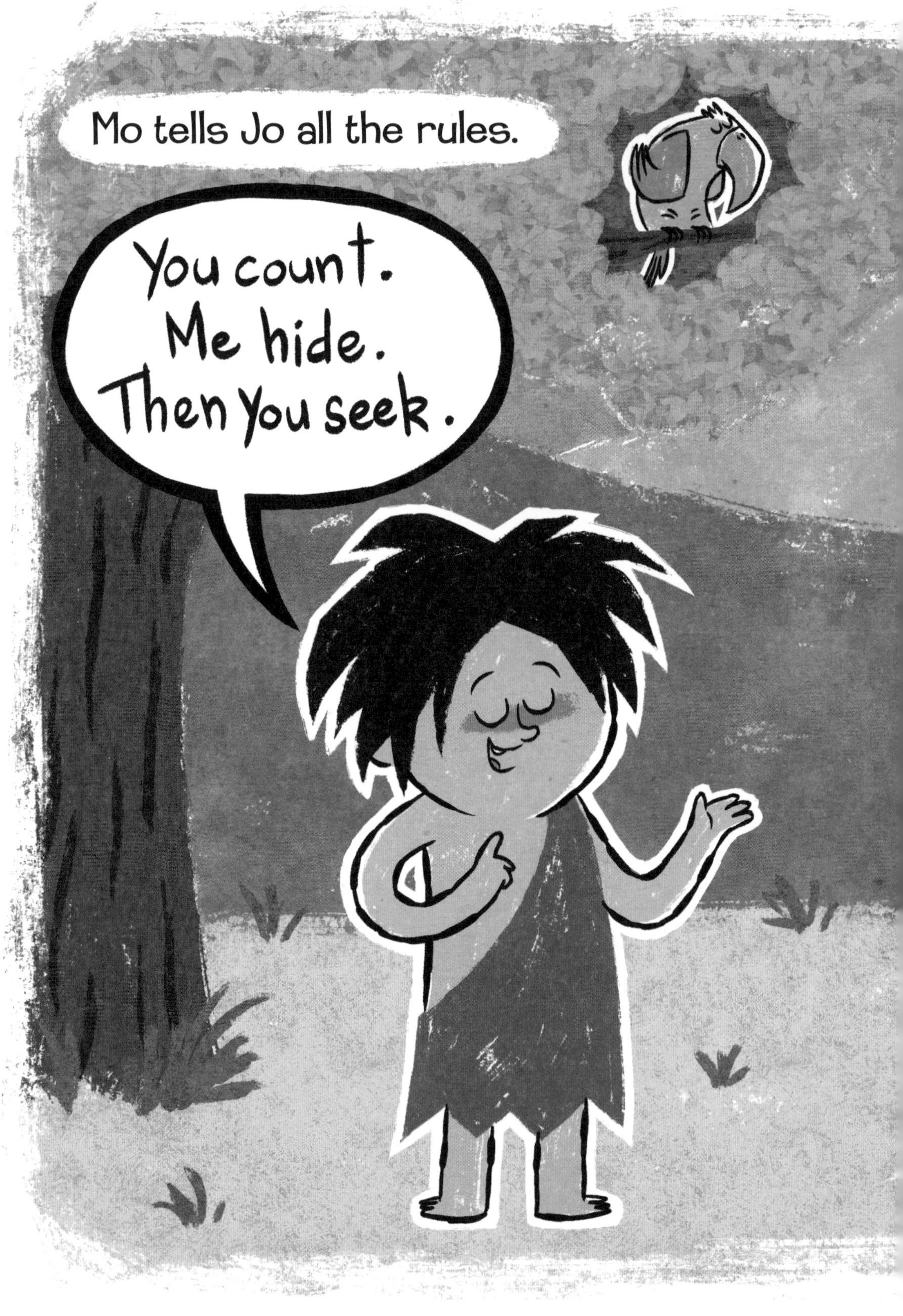
Mo tells Jo all the rules.
You count. Me hide. Then You seek.

Now Mo can't find Jo!

Who will win the game?

Mo and Jo want to warm up.

Need fire.
Need wood!

Mo and Jo try to make fire.

Mo has a new idea.

Mo and Jo think and think.
How can they get warm?

Jo sees some birds.
The birds do not look cold.

Mo and Jo find feathers.
Is this a good idea?

Mo and Jo find leaves.

Jo and Mo see a bear.
The bear doesn't look cold.

How can Mo and Jo get some fur?
Mo and Jo try to pull the fur.

This is not a good idea.

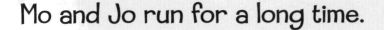

Mo and Jo run for a long time.

Me not cold!

Running make warm!

Mo and Jo sit down to rest.

But now they are cold again! So...

The End

Welcome to a new series created to cross the bridge between "read-to-me" books and "read-on-my-own" books!

Discover a series of books created to help new readers move from simple picture books to the challenges of chapter books. These engaging stories are between 72 and 96 pages in length, but with just a few words on each page—while the page count increases, the word count remains low.

Best of all, each of the books features fresh-and-funny characters. Kids will feel like they've made some great new friends who reflect their lives and feelings.

Downloadable activity and discussion materials for kids, parents, and educators are available on the Blue Apple Books website: **www.blueapplebooks.com**.